THIS BLOOMSBURY BOOK

BELONGS TO

....

To Princess
Iris Harper Haynes
K. L.

To my sisters
S. H.

Bloomsbury Publishing, London, Berlin and New York

First published in Great Britain in 2010 by Bloomsbury Publishing Plc
36 Soho Square, London, W1D 3QY

A CIP catalogue record of this book is available from the British Library

ISBN 978 0 7475 9929 6

Printed in China

1 3 5 7 9 10 8 6 4 2

All papers used by Bloomsbury Publishing are natural, recyclable products made
from wood grown in well-managed forests. The manufacturing processes conform
to the environmental regulations of the country of origin

www.bloomsbury.com/childrens

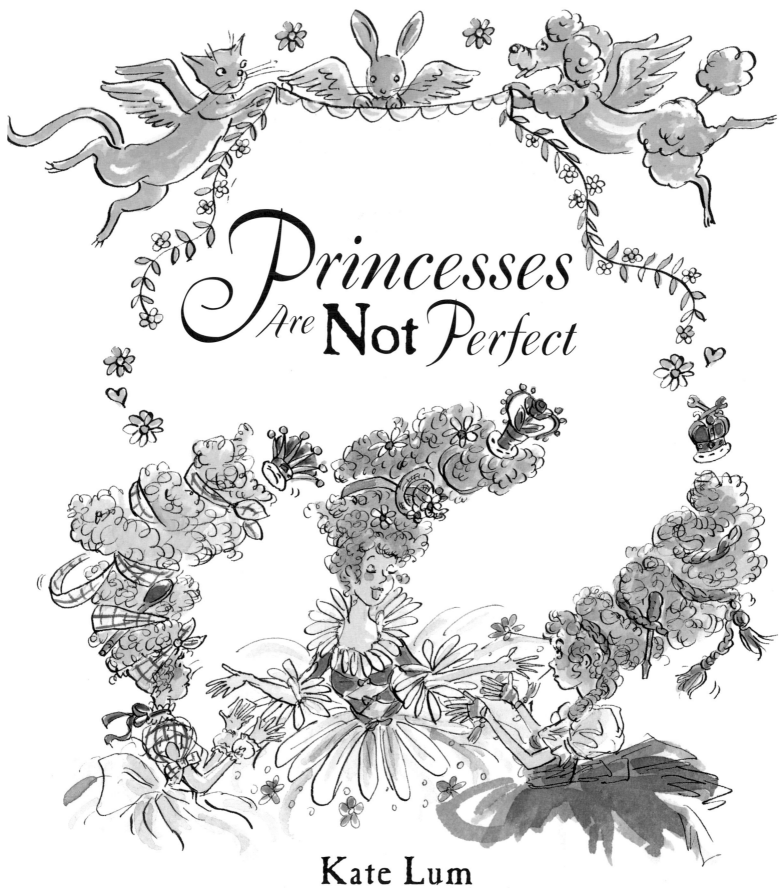

Princesses Are Not Perfect

Kate Lum

Illustrated by Sue Hellard

BLOOMSBURY

LONDON BERLIN NEW YORK

Once there were three princesses:
Princess Allie, Princess Mellie and Princess Libby.
They lived in a rose-covered palace by the sea.

They weren't the kind of princesses who sit around doing nothing.

They were very busy.

They grew things in the garden,
they baked things in the bakehouse
and they built things in the workshop.

Each princess had her speciality.

Princess Allie **loved** to **bake.**
She made the best cakes you've
ever tasted, covered with
royal decorations.
When she baked, she
felt completely happy.

Princess Libby **loved** to **build things.**
If you wanted anything made, Princess Libby
was the person to ask. When she was
hammering, she didn't think
about anything else.

Pig Palace

Recipe
Royal
Icing

Princess Mellie **loved** her **garden.**
She could make just about anything
grow, no matter what the weather.
When she gardened, she felt all was
right with the world.

One sunny morning, the princesses were sitting
in the palace dining room having breakfast.
They were making plans. The next day, all the
children in the princessdom were coming
to the palace for the Summer Party.

Suddenly
Princess Mellie,
who had not slept very well, said,
'I don't see why I always have to be the one to garden.'

The other princesses looked at her in surprise.

'Garden, garden, all day long,' complained Mellie.
'Dirt here, weeds there. I am sick and tired of it.'

'Well, what would you like
to do instead?' asked Allie.

'Bake!' said Mellie. 'I want to bake things.
I'm sure I can bake just as well as you.
Princesses are good at everything.'

'But if you bake, what will
I do?' cried Allie.

'You could **build
things**,' said Mellie.
'And Libby could **garden**.
Don't you ever get bored, doing
the same jobs again and again?'

'Well, yes . . . once in a while,'
said Allie and Libby.

'Then it's all settled!' cried Mellie.
'I'm the baker, Allie is the builder and Libby is
the gardener. I'm sure that everything we do will be perfect.'

As soon as they had
finished eating, they ran
to see the housekeeper,
Mrs Blue.

'Mrs Blue,' they announced, 'we are switching jobs. From now on, Allie will be the builder. If you want anything made, go to her. Mellie will be the baker. If we need any treats, let her know. And Libby will be the gardener. Go to her for fruits and flowers.'

Mrs Blue looked worried. 'Yes, Your Princesses,' she said. 'But do you think this is a good idea?'

'Of course, Mrs Blue,' said Allie, Mellie and Libby. *'Princesses are good at everything.'*

'Very well,' said Mrs Blue. 'Tomorrow is the Summer Party for all the children in the princessdom. We will need 100 small baskets of berries.' 'No problem, Mrs Blue,' said Libby.

'We will need 100 cupcakes with pink roses,' said Mrs Blue. 'No problem, Mrs Blue,' said Mellie.

'We will need 100 little chairs,' said Mrs Blue. 'No problem, Mrs Blue,' said Allie.

So Princess Mellie went into the bakehouse.
She looked at the bags of flour and sugar.
She looked at the barrels of fruits and nuts.

'Easy as pie!' said Princess Mellie.

And she set to work.

Princess Allie went to the workshop. She looked
at the piles of wood and nails. She looked at the
hammers and the planes and the saws.

'How hard can this be?' asked Princess Allie.
And she set to work.

Princess Libby went out to the garden. She looked
at the hoses and the shovels and the trowels.

'Nothing to it,' said Princess Libby.
And she set to work.

Several hours later, Princess Libby
had **picked**
the blueberries.

Princess Allie had **built** the chairs.

Princess Mellie had **baked** the cupcakes.

The three princesses limped into the dining room. Mrs Blue had prepared a delicious supper, but none of them felt like eating.

'How did the building go?' asked Princess Libby.
'Perfectly,' snapped Princess Allie.

'How did the gardening go?' asked Princess Mellie.

'No problem,' insisted Princess Libby.

'Princesses are good at everything.'

'And what about the baking?' wondered Princess Allie.

'Easy,' said Princess Mellie.

'Princesses are good at everything.'

And with that, the three princesses went off to bed.

Princess Allie couldn't sleep.

She **rolled** this way
and she **rolled** that way.

She **sighed**
loudly.

She **rubbed** her tired feet.

There is only **one** *thing that will cheer me up,*
thought Princess Allie at last. *And that is a good
bout of* **baking!** So she got up, put on her royal
robe and sneaked out to the bakehouse.

Meanwhile, in her room, Princess Libby couldn't sleep. She **stretched** and **yawned**.

She **brushed** her hair.

She **brushed** her dog.

Finally, she gave up.

'There is only **one** thing that will cheer me up,' said Princess Libby. 'And that is a good hour with my **tools!**'

So she got up, put on her royal robe and sneaked out to the workshop.

Poor Princess Mellie couldn't sleep either.

She **tried** counting sheep.

She **tried** counting goats.

She **tried** drinking cocoa.

Nothing helped.

'The **only** thing that will make me feel better is to spend some time in my **garden**,' sighed Princess Mellie.

So she got up, put on her royal robe
and sneaked out to the gardens.

The next morning, all three princesses were late to breakfast. But all three princesses were smiling.

'I had a wonderful night!' declared Libby.

'Best night I've ever had,' smiled Mellie.

'Yes, it was perfect,' laughed Allie.

They ate breakfast quickly and ran upstairs, to be dressed and ready for the children's Summer Party.

By noon, 100 children had arrived. They played games,
ran races and splashed in the sea. Then Mrs Blue
ushered them all into a giant tent.

It was decorated with roses,
golden plates
and piles of treats.

Everything was perfect, except . . .

'Where are the chairs?' cried Mrs Blue.

'Here they are, Mrs Blue!'
laughed Princess Libby.
And she wheeled in 100 perfect little chairs.

Princess Allie stared.

'And where are the blueberries?' wondered Mrs Blue.

'Here we go!' cried Princess Mellie.
And she brought in 100 baskets of lovely blueberries.

Princess Libby stared.

'And what about the cupcakes?'
reminded Mrs Blue.

'No problem!' called Princess Allie.
And she carried in 100 perfect cupcakes.

Princess Mellie stared.

The children were very happy. They sat in the chairs,
they munched the berries and they loved the cupcakes.

'Princesses make great things,' said one
little girl. 'How can they do so much?'

'That's easy,' said another girl.
'Princesses are good at everything.'

The princesses looked at each other. Then they started to laugh.

'Princesses,' said Princess Allie, 'are **good** at what they **love.** You **don't** have to be **good** at **everything** to be a princess.'

'That is very true, Your Princesses,' said Mrs Blue. 'Very true indeed!'

Once there were three princesses . . .

Join Allie, Mellie and Libby
in an enchanting tale of role reversal
by Kate Lum and illustrated by Sue Hellard

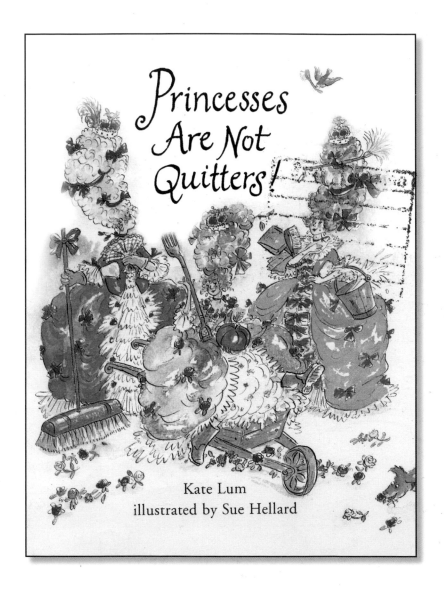

'Funny and original, comical and addictive'
Sunday Times